Dedication

Amidst the symphony of thoughts, this book hums a melody
dedicated to my dear father's loving memory

THE LEGEND OF ICARUS

FLIGHT OF DESTINY:
UNVEILING THE MYTHICAL ODYSSEY

JITSPEED

INDIA • SINGAPORE • MALAYSIA

Jitspeed's "The Legend of Icarus" is a remarkable novel that transports readers to a world of magic and wonder. His writing is vivid and engaging, and his characters are complex and relatable. I was particularly impressed by the author's spiritual insights, which he incorporates into the story in a way that is both natural and meaningful. "The Legend of Icarus" is a story that will stay with you long after you finish reading it. I highly recommend it to readers of all ages.

Dr. K JayanthMurali
Retired DGP | Corporate Strategy and Security Consultant |
Peak performance and Wellness Coach for Executives |
Marathon Runner | Author

***

The book "The Legend of Icarus - Flight of Destiny: Unveiling the Mythical Odyssey" is a fantastic fictional book that takes any reader on a magical journey of mystery and mythology. You made an effort in terms of bringing the fantastic elements that help a reader navigate through the fictional adventure. It's an extraordinary journey filled with whimsy and wonder in every phase of the book. Each page is a feast for the eyes, enhancing the storytelling experience and adding an extra layer of magic to the narrative. I wholeheartedly recommend the book to children. It's a literary gem that sparks imagination, fosters a love for reading, and imparts creativity. It's both entertaining and educational. Thank you, JitSpeed, for creating a masterpiece at the age of 9 years and it will be treasured for generations to come.

Mubeen Irshad
Incubated @ IIMB NSRCEL | Author of Book "Positive Ripples" |
Transformed 500 plus children into Authors and Speakers |
Touched 10000 people through Training |Purpose Coach |
Certified Corporate Trainer | Storyteller

Contents

Acknowledgment

This is for my amazing mother, who has been my biggest support throughout my life. She's been the source of my motivation and happiness, always pushing me to keep moving forward. She's not just the greatest mother in my world, but she's also been my rock through so many situations. She understands me like no one else and is truly the most lovable mother in the whole world. So, thank you Amma! I also want to express my deepest gratitude to my father because he's been just as instrumental in helping me. Thank you, Appa!

Introduction

In the ancient tapestries of mythology, a figure of legend emerges, veiled in mystery and graced with extraordinary abilities. Stories of this reputed, famous being have echoed through time, fascinating the minds of all who have encountered their accomplishments. From the heart of the charming woodlands, to the lofty peaks of the celestial mountains, this mysterious entity ventures into grand quests, facing both bitter foes and a formidable three-headed beast. An incarnation of bravery, wisdom, and determination, this imaginary champion shines as a guiding light of hope and inspiration, leaving a permanent mark with their remarkable character. Join me on an odyssey of marvels as I unravel the enthralling saga of this exceptional hero, the saviour of an entire cosmos.

Chapter 1

An Unexpected Encounter

"**W**ell, here I stand. They call me Icarus, not to be confused with the wax-winged figure from Greek mythology! If you're wondering how I ended up here, allow me to explain. It all started when I was just a young boy living in the New York city. It was a lively party and I was amusing myself until my uncle Taurus approached with urgency in his voice. "Come with me," he said, "your father is levitating."

I ridiculed at first, thinking it to be a joke, until I witnessed it myself. There he was, my father, suspended in the air. A voice was menacing and other-worldly echo was heard, "Aquarius, RETURN YOUR PROMISE."

My father was trembling and responded, "Alright, Mytro, I will do as you ask." Suddenly, a surge of power coursed through me and with a hesitant punch, I managed to repel the beast back to its empire. I hoped it would be the end of it. But, little did I know, fate had a different plan in store for me."

Chapter 2
Spirits Speak Truth

Following the incident, the revelry came to a halt and I sought rest on my couch, attempting to clear my mind of the recent events. Upon waking, my uncle Taurus and father exclaimed in astonishment, "HOW DID YOU DO THAT?" I retorted, "I DON'T KNOW, OKAY!" in a raised voice, prompting them to leave me be for a while. Eventually, my uncle returned, urging, "Come with me, I have something to show you. "We entered his car and ventured to an unfamiliar location. When I inquired, he explained it was a site for awakening elemental powers. A question of doubt lingered in my mind, but against my instincts, I chose to trust him.

Exiting the car, we were greeted by fire-wielding monks who bestowed their blessings upon me. We reached our destination: a training ground. My uncle disclosed that many generations back, our ancestors, had been friends with these monks. I remarked, "Wow, then I'm eager to begin training." He agreed, leading me to meet their leader. Though baffled, as soon as the leader laid eyes on me, he revealed, "You are perfect. You shall become a fire master." Introducing himself as Infernation, I exclaimed saying, "An incredible name, sir." He graciously replied, "Thank you."

From that point on, he diligently instructed me in every facet of fire manipulation, from the fundamental techniques to the most advanced skills. Upon completing my training, the fire master declared, "You already possessed mastery over fire before you arrived here. I knew you were destined for greatness." On being puzzled, I sought clarification. But, he departed without providing an answer, leaving me with these confusing words: "Since you've mastered fire, I shall reveal the next element to conquer. It is fire's natural opponent."

Bidding him farewell, we returned to the car and departed. Turning to my uncle, I inquired, "How do you know all of this?" He responded, "When you were a baby, both your father and I, along with your mother, saw a mark upon you. We recognized it as the mark of the chosen one." Gazing into the mirror, I discovered a distinctive mark upon my forehead. I asked, "Who is the chosen one?" He explained, "The chosen one is the individual who attains mastery over all elements, balances all chakras, and excels in weaponry." I remarked, "Well, it seems we have a long journey ahead of us." So, my uncle and I embarked on our next pilgrimage to an awakening ground of power.

Chapter 3

Unbelievable! The Chosen One with One Element

Upon arriving at our next destination, we entered the premises only to be met with a stern warning, "You mustn't proceed, for you possess the forbidden element." Startled, I asked, "What is this forbidden element?" Their response: "It is fire." My disbelief surged, "But I was blessed by fire monks and have mastered its art. I am the chosen one, yet you bar my way?" Their murmurs of apology followed, assuring me, "Sorry, sir. We shall permit your entry." Though baffled, I went ahead.

Inside, I encountered a prominent figure who introduced himself as Hydroka, the water leader. Despite my proficiency in fire, including the forbidden element, he graciously consented to instruct me in the ways of water. I was thrilled, embarking on a journey from the basics to the most advanced techniques. Once again, I had triumphed in mastering another element.

Stepping outside the boundaries, I tested my newfound abilities, first with fire, then water. It felt nothing short of magical. Summoning my uncle to join me in the car, he commended, "Icarus, you are the most remarkable elemental apprentice in the world." Grateful, I replied, "Thank you for the praise. But, now we must strive to master all elements before midnight, which is a personal challenge. Having conquered fire and water, I aim to progress even faster. Let us press on." So, we sped towards the next power awakening area, the domain of earth.

Chapter 4

A Pioneering Encounter with Earth

As we hastened towards the next power awakening site, hunger bit me hard. We stopped for lunch, and I reassured my parents of my safety. After our meal, we resumed our journey. Just before we arrived, my uncle offered a solemn caution: "Icarus, are you certain you'll be alright in this territory? Earth is an immensely mighty element, and if you unintentionally provoke a master, they could trigger an earthquake. Please, assure me that you'll exercise caution." I affirmed, "Rest assured, Uncle. Just because I've mastered previous elements doesn't mean I'll be reckless here."

Despite the anxiety caused; no calamity happened to us. Spotting earth monks in meditation, my keen eyesight recognized the leader. He marvelled, "You spotted me from the ground. May I inspect your forehead for a moment?" I consented. Upon seeing the mark, he gasped, "You are the chosen one! How many elements have you mastered?" I confessed, "Only two." When he asked which, I admitted, "Fire and water, though they aren't known to be compatible." He nodded, "Indeed, they aren't, just as earth doesn't readily mix with either fire or water. Let's commence your training in the earth element." I inquired, "By the way, what's your name?" He responded, "I am Ercus." I commended, "A fine name." He offered no verbal reply. Rather merely gave me a warm smile.

Though more challenging than its predecessors, I eventually conquered the earth element. The leader announced, "You have now mastered three elements. The fourth is air, a name akin to mine. He's my brother, in fact, we're all siblings." Departing the area, a sense of accomplishment escorted us. I asked my uncle for the time, and he informed me it was 2:00 PM. I breathed a sigh of relief, grateful it wasn't the eve or midnight. It then struck me that 2 o'clock was post-sunset. Nonetheless, I took solace in having completed my earth training.

Upon returning home, I recounted the day's events to my parents. Initially unconvinced, they witnessed my abilities and, over time, came to accept them. Satisfied, I retired for the night, eager for the adventures that awaited me on the morrow.

Chapter 5

Elemental Mastery: Unleashing My Newfound Powers

The whole eventuality took an unexpected turn as I discovered my newfound abilities to control the elements. Starting early at 7 AM, I embarked on the journey with my uncle to the next power awakening area, which focused on air. Meeting the leader, Arcus, was a warm welcome. However, during training, I inadvertently summoned a tornado, prompting Arcus to swiftly guide us to shelter. Once the storm passed, I resumed training and eventually mastered the element. Arcus then presented me with glasses to shield against the potent Myria Violet.

Moving forward, I arrived at the next area and encountered a mysterious figure on the street. To my surprise, she revealed herself as Astraea, claiming to be the sister of someone named Icarus. I disclosed my identity, leaving her astonished. Astraea shared her interests, including a love for chess and mathematics, and warned about the Myria Violet illusion. We sought guidance from the real leader, Lycire, who granted permission for training.

After rigorous training, I achieved mastery over the light element. Introducing Astraea to my uncle led to an amusing accident. We had a heart-to-heart about her life in hiding, evading the government's pursuit of her superpower. Her stay at Fountain Houses was arranged by our parents. Witnessing the reunion between my parents and Astraea was a profound

moment. She opted to stay with them, allowing me to continue my adventure.

In a revealing conversation with my uncle, I learned he had shielded her for a decade. The next destination introduced me to Necrospirit, a leader whose intimidating name contrasted with his kind attitude. Mastering the art of shadow, I left the area and returned home, eager for some well-deserved rest.

Chapter 6

Unleashing the Inner Energy

Upon reaching our destination, a sacred temple, I entered and greeted the monks and the wise sage. Curious, the sage inquired about my purpose. "I've come to awaken my chakras," I replied. The sage questioned, "Why do you seek to awaken them?" With conviction, I proclaimed, "I am the chosen one, that is why." The sage was taken aback by this revelation and graciously allowed me into a meditative chamber, where not a single sound could be heard.

As I closed my eyes, a door appeared before me, bearing the inscription "Root Chakra." Inside, I beheld a withering plant and a brimming watering can. I tenderly poured the water, and the plant exploded into a colossal tree. Soon, a myriad of creatures sought refuge beneath its branches, drawn by their own purpose. Another door materialized, revealing the "Sacral Chakra."

Inside, a lively boy skittered about. Amongst the table, pen, and paper, he crafted a drawing—a portrait of my family. Surprised, I queried, "How do you know of my family, young one?" To which he responded, "I know everything about you. I am not a child, but a guardian." In a radiant transformation, the child assumed a guardian-like form. The next door materialized, marked "Solar Plexus Chakra."

Stepping through, I witnessed an illusion of my family engaged in a conversation my sister would rather keep private, hidden from both me and the world. When the illusion dissolved, I met my sister, knowing every detail about her was now unveiled. A quaking sensation led me to the door labelled "Heart Chakra." Doubts arose—what if my loved ones were left with nothing? Repeating, "This is not real," I yearned for their embrace. Yet, devoid of sensation, I knew it was but an illusion.

The rumbling returned as the door marked "Throat Chakra" beckoned. Struggling to speak, I waited in vain as another voice took precedence. Impatience took hold, and I cried out, "COME ON, YOU CAN'T EVEN LET SOMEONE SPEAK AFTER SO LONG!" Silence fell, replaced by a peculiar door adorned with three eyes—a mere illusion.

Beyond it lay a wondrous chamber, adorned with stars, galaxies, and celestial bodies. A voice queried, "Will you forge on or choose another path?" Resolute, I replied, "I must press on." Ascending ten steps, each brought greater tranquillity. The tenth step ushered profound relief, washing away all turmoil and sorrow. A white door awaited, signifying enlightenment. The stairs, I realized, were a mere facet of the Crown Chakra.

Upon awakening, I found my uncle nearby, unaware of my absence. Departing the meditation chamber, I sought out the others. In a nearby dwelling, I shared my journey. Initially baffled, they later came to accept my tale. Rest was well-deserved, and I slumbered, knowing that my meditation had borne fruit.

Chapter 7

The Might of Blades

After a brief respite, I returned to the car and made my way to a dojo that housed an impressive array of swords. Upon reaching our destination, I stepped out of the car, greeted by curious faces inquiring about my identity. I confidently revealed myself as the chosen one, which left them visibly astonished. I couldn't help but ask, "What's the cause of your surprise?" They responded, "Because you bear the dragon mark, the insignia of the chosen one." I gazed at myself in a nearby mirror, remarking, "Well, I must say, having a dragon mark is rather impressive."

They proceeded to inform me that they would bestow upon me a katana known as the Omniverse katana (sword), a weapon said to be manageable by only two individuals: the chosen one and the Supreme god. Intrigued, I inquired about the Omniverse and the identity of the Supreme god. Their explanation revealed that the Omniverse encompasses all planets, galaxies, and universes, and that the Supreme god is a celestial and divine entity credited with its creation.

After this enlightening conversation, I took hold of the katana and marvelled at its potency, which was demonstrated when it shattered the dojo floor. They assured me it would be repaired, but I opted to employ my earth-controlling abilities to mend it myself. With the floor restored, I resumed my training.

Before my departure, they informed me that I was obliged to partake in a duel. I agreed, and my initial adversary proved to be inept with a sword, resulting in my repeated victories. They then presented me with a more formidable challenger, whom I also overcame. This pattern continued, with each opponent growing progressively stronger. Even the masters themselves eventually stepped up, but I emerged victorious against them all. With no further challengers remaining, they released me.

I returned to the car and made my way home, craving some well-deserved rest after the exhausting period.

Chapter 8

Astraea Gazes Up at the Stars

This chapter is dedicated to my extraordinary sister. She embodies greatness in every sense. Possessing a wealth of knowledge, she has a genuine fondness for interacting with the public. Her interests span across a multitude of subjects, a testament to her remarkable intellect. Beyond that, she possesses an exceptional moral compass, earning her the title of a truly good-hearted individual. Among her exceptional attributes, she wields a unique power known as the Astro Sword. This awe-inspiring weapon is adorned with stars, galaxies, planets, and the entire universe, making it a sight to behold. It also summons a suit of armour, offering both protection and a formidable presence when the need arises.

In her youth, my sister exhibited a mischievous streak, a trait that added a dash of excitement to her character. Interestingly, her name pays homage to the Greek God of Justice, a fitting nickname as she always seeks to uphold what is right. Her affinity for stargazing and contemplating the vastness of space reveals her innate curiosity about the universe.

Moreover, she boasts incredible physical prowess. During her training sessions, she demonstrated a remarkable display of strength by effortlessly shattering wood, iron, and other formidable materials. This power was nothing short of astounding. As a testament to her achievements, my sister's collection includes a multitude of well-deserved medals and trophies.

And with that, I conclude this chapter."

Chapter 9

Unravelling the Mystery

"**A**fter a much-needed rest at home, I ventured outside for a leisurely stroll. Along the way, I observed people going about their everyday activities. As I turned onto the main street, where the city bustled with life, an ominous voice boomed, demanding, "Hello mortal, how did you manage to strike me?"

I inquired, "Firstly, who are you? What is your name?" The voice identified itself as Mytro. I pressed further, "So you're the one. What is it that you seek? What pact did you make with him?"

The monstrous entity revealed, "Long before your existence, I swore an oath that when he bore a child, that child would meet its end at my hands." I challenged, "Face me like the true monster you claim to be."

He retorted, "No, mortal. You must come to me. Take heed, for many have fallen in their futile attempts against me. Train harder than ever before, or your own lifeless form will be displayed before your father." I scoffed at the threat, declaring, "You underestimate me. I am the chosen one. I've mastered all elements, harmonized all Chakras, and wield expertise in weaponry. You stand no chance, not even in infinite lifetimes."

The creature warned, "We will face each other soon. But mark my words, train and fight, or you will meet your demise." I vowed, "When that day comes, I will display all three of your heads once they've been broken, for I believe you possess three."

With mocking laughter, the monster's voice faded, leaving me to hasten home. I recounted the encounter to my astonished family, who were more shocked than ever before. As night fell, I struggled to sleep, their voices intermingling, until, over time, we all grew accustomed to it.

In a dream, I revisited the figure who introduced me to a concept called the 'creation blast.' By prioritizing destructive elements, then merging them with others, I achieved a powerful explosion. Conversely, prioritizing creative elements yielded wondrous results, like the manifestation of a luminous, flying angel. Upon testing, it proved real, akin to magic. After a day filled with chores and experiments, I finally found solace in slumber.

Chapter 10

The Ascent of the Supreme god

As the sun greeted the day, I found myself on that familiar street, but this time, it wasn't Mytro, the monstrous entity.

A divine voice resonated, asking, "Greetings, what is your desire?" I countered, "First, who are you?" He revealed himself as Supreme god. I was taken aback, face to face with the architect of the Omniverse, conversing with an ordinary person with superhuman abilities. He then revealed that he was the one who had instructed me about the 'creation blast' in my dream. We engaged in a profound conversation, discussing his existence and the challenges he faced. It became clear he needed my assistance in vanquishing my enemy, Mytro.

I questioned, "Why seek my aid when you possess such immense power?" He explained, "For if I were to intervene directly, I would break a solemn vow—to safeguard all the universes." I suggested, "Could you not create duplicates of yourself to aid across the world, being the creator?" He countered, "They wouldn't sense my presence. I must physically be there for them to feel it. Now, let us deliberate our course of action."

He outlined, "You must first defeat the monster and demonstrate to the world that it has been vanquished. However, this is only the beginning. You must ascend to the highest reaches of the Omniverse Temple, for the monster is immortal. It is there that you must confront him once more." I inquired about the temple's appearance. He described it as a colossal edifice adorned with designs of stars, galaxies, planets, and every facet of the Omniverse. I pressed, "Where can it be found?" He revealed that it lay in a distant realm, the land of Ashura, reachable only through traversing mountains, seas, storms, and deserts—a formidable journey indeed.

Our discourse concluded, he imparted, "Your path is set. You may call upon me at any time. Simply visit the same alley and speak my name, and I shall be there." With that, his voice fell silent, and I returned home, the evening already upon us. One more rest awaited me before the dawn of a new day.

Chapter 11

The Preparations for the Epic Battle in the Omniverse

Upon awakening, I noticed that the chosen mark on my forehead had transformed. Instead, I now bore intricate serpentine patterns in shades of blue and red, twirling and intertwining on my arm. Turning to my sister, I inquired, "What is this?" She replied, "I believe you've been blessed by the Supreme god." Puzzled, I asked, "Why me?" My sister speculated, "Perhaps it's because you spoke to the monster. Just a guess."

"How did you know?" I pressed, but my uncle interjected, alerting us to a visitor outside. Stepping out, I heard that same divine voice greeting me, "Hello Icarus, how are you?" I responded with a smile, and he, understanding, joined us inside. The Supreme god suggested I address him as Sornia for brevity. We delved into discussions about Zynors and their elemental affinities. As a practitioner of fire, water, air, light, earth, and shadow, I shared my journey with him.

After our conversation, I bid farewell to my uncle and the Supreme god. While returning back, I recounted our discussion to my uncle, detailing the weapons, the journey, and much more. We sought refuge in an obscure hotel for the night. Our quest for the elusive land of Ashura led us to ask locals, but no one could provide answers until we encountered an individual who possessed comprehensive knowledge of the journey ahead. He outlined a treacherous path through the

Saharian Desert, Poseidon's Wrath Sea, Warnius's rocky terrain, Tornadius's stormy regions, the radiant Astronome, and the lightless Umbrender. When I queried, "How do we navigate these challenges?" He replied, "Only with the aid of the Zynors."

Determined, I set out to locate the building housing the Zynors. It took hours of tireless searching, but eventually, we discovered it. Guarded with utmost vigilance, only those with a pass were permitted entry. Resorting to the vents, I accessed the chamber. Within, the Zynors were divided into distinct trials. They first demanded a test of agility, assessing one's jumping prowess. Negotiating spikes, ramps, and springs, I claimed the first Zynor. Passing it to my uncle for safekeeping, a robotic voice instructed, "You've passed the first test. Proceed to the second."

The second trial began promptly, pushing me to run at full tilt. Evading projectiles and automated adversaries, I secured the water weapon and delivered it to my uncle. The voice announced, "You're exceptional. On to the third test." Emerging, a robot appeared from the ground. I challenged it with my mental abilities, igniting fire, manipulating air, wielding earth, ensnaring with shadow and blinding with light. The robot succumbed in a blaze of glory, yielding the air weapon. After passing it to my uncle, the voice directed, "Press on to the fourth."

In the fourth challenge, I engaged in a cerebral showdown with a robot. Progressing through levels of increasing complexity, I prevailed swiftly, drawing on knowledge acquired from my earlier years. The fifth level delved into advanced subjects, yet I emerged triumphant, securing the fourth weapon. The voice remarked, "Impressive, but onward to the fifth and final test."

The last trial introduced a cyborg, seemingly meditating. I adopted my own meditative stance and focused on the 'Om chant.' The cyborg faltered, dispatched from the arena. Claiming the fifth weapon, I handed it to my uncle. The voice lauded, "You're a true champion. Will you accept the prize?" With certainty, I affirmed, "Yes, I will." The robot declared, "We have a new winner!"

Returning, I inspected my newly acquired weapons. The fiery sword emanated a blazing aura, capable of igniting wood, stone, and iron. The water and earth daggers exuded a unique charm. The air and shadow spears boasted remarkable range, while the light mace exuded its own brilliance. Each weapon found its place in a specially designed box, which I amalgamated into a single container. It fit snugly in the back of our vehicle.

Seeking respite within my home, I indulged in a long and much-needed rest. The trials, weapon acquisition, and extensive travel had left me utterly exhausted.

Chapter 12

The Omniverse War

As I awoke, I found Sornia in my presence, having just finished a conversation with my sister. She expressed her desire to join our cause, armed with her formidable abilities. I was well aware of her strengths and she also suggested adding one more person to our team. Sornia agreed, emphasizing the need for someone either closely connected to Icarus or someone whose skills would be invaluable. And so, they embarked on a quest to locate this crucial addition.

Sornia scoured every nook of The Omniverse, while my sister combed through the universes and multiverses, each bringing their own unique perspective. Sornia had an uncanny ability to unearth the tiniest details, be they possible or impossible, whereas my sister's vision was attuned to the broader spectrum of possibilities. After an exhaustive search, they discovered a person named Xzrono. Pronouncing his name was a challenge, but I managed. He proved to be a formidable force, possessing both incredible combat prowess and intellectual acumen. He knew every strategic nuance across the Omniverse and could discern an opponent's vulnerabilities.

As we gathered in the car, my parents had somehow slipped in. I briefed them on the impending battle, and they were taken aback. After the initial shock subsided, I queried them about their roles in the upcoming conflict. My father possessed the ability to halt time, while my mother wielded an even darker form of magic. I suggested that my father freeze time when I engaged the monster, enabling me to

The Omniverse War

deliver relentless blows. However, I emphasized that time should only stand still for the monster, leaving the temple and everything else unaffected. Meanwhile, my mother's dark magic would bestow me with a distinct advantage in the battle.

My uncle inquired about the weaponry. I directed him to the back of the car, emphasizing that we were entering the treacherous realm of Warnius. When I called for the car to halt, he asked why. I explained that it was time to lay out the plan and retrieve the weapons. He acquiesced, and I proceeded to outline our strategy.

My sister would take her position atop the temple, awaiting my signal. Once I brought the monster's incapacitated form to the temple, she would seal off all entrances. Then, I would unleash a relentless assault on the creature. My father's temporal abilities would ensure that the monster remained motionless, allowing me to strike with exemption. After a concerted onslaught, my mother would amplify my strengths with her dark magic. Subsequently, my sister would join the fray, employing her powers against the monster. Meanwhile, Xzrono would discern the creature's vulnerabilities.

They all applauded the plan, but my uncle sought his role. I asked about his abilities, learning he possessed strength beyond measure. I dubbed it an amplified version of superhuman strength, enlisting him to join the fray when my sister initiated her assault.

With the plan in place, we set off on our journey, eventually arriving at the daunting expanse of Poseidon's Wrath. A boat large enough to accommodate a car was our means of passage. Contemplating my powers, I realized I could create a water path to traverse the ocean safely. It proved to be a smooth journey, and I felt an unfamiliar surge of happiness.

Approaching the rocky terrain of Warnius, I instinctively erected a shield to guard against potential rockslides. Surprisingly, none materialized, and we safely traversed the area. Our path led us through the stormy regions of Tornadius, where every lightning strike seemed to seek us out. Finally, we emerged from that tumultuous domain.

As we searched for Astronome, a brilliant light engulfed us, prompting me to wield the mace. Spinning it, I gradually dispelled the blinding radiance, revealing the landscape in its true form. We pressed on, encountering the remnants of past adventurers, hinting that this may have been Mytro's former abode. I speculated he had relocated due to the perpetual darkness.

Upon reaching the temple, I took my position at the front entrance. My sister ascended to a vantage point, while my parents and uncle assumed their designated posts. It was unclear if the monster lurked inside, but upon a cautious peek, I confirmed its presence. Through Morse code, I relayed the message to my allies, even reaching my distant parents.

The battle ensued, and Mytro taunted us with disrespect. Undeterred, I unleashed my elemental powers, igniting the floor and summoning torrents of water. Though I struggled, I persisted, resorting to liftoff. My attacks seemed ineffectual and then, as he grew 7 more heads, it felt like all hope was slipping away. Each head seemed to possess its own special ability - one for fire, one for water, one for earth, one for air, one for light, one for shadow, one for mental power, one for physical, and one for spiritual. It became so overwhelming and I couldn't help but feel like I had let him down until my sister struck Mytro with a decisive blow. My father froze time, allowing us to thrash the monster relentlessly. My mother's dark magic heightened my strength, rendering me formidable.

Amidst the melee, Xzrono discerned Mytro's weakness. I rallied my energy and unleashed a devastating Creation Blast. Mytro appeared weakened, and with renewed vigor, I proceeded to dismantle his heads, aided by my sister. In a final act, we vanquished him, scattering his remains far from Earth. The remaining ashes met their end in a pool of molten lava, sealing Mytro's fate.

Sornia bid us farewell, ascending into the sky, while Xzrono sought refuge in my home. Exhausted yet victorious, we returned home, each moment etched in our memories.

The END